A MASKED
FAIRY TALE

Little Red RIDING HOOD

Illustrated by Ellie Jenkins

Kane Miller
A DIVISION OF EDC PUBLISHING

ONCE UPON A TIME,

there was a young girl named Little Red Riding Hood.

Three of her FAVORITE things were:

1) Long walks in the forest,
2) Visiting her grandma (who lived in the forest), <u>AND</u>
3) Carrying baskets JAM-PACKED with tasty goodies.

On this day, Little Red Riding Hood was doing ALL of her favorite things at once.

Little Red Riding Hood was a CLEVER and KIND girl,
but she had a dreadful singing voice.

"TRA-LA-LA!
I'M OFF TO SEE MY POOR,
SICK GRANDMA!
LA-LA-LA!"

Little Red Riding Hood sang as she skipped.

A wolf stepped out from behind a tree.

"Oh, what a lovely singing voice!"
he lied, licking his lips greedily. **"Do you need help carrying
that basket full of delicious-looking goodies?"**

Little Red Riding Hood narrowed her eyes. If there was one thing
she knew, it was NEVER TRUST A HUNGRY WOLF,
EVER!

"I don't need any help, thank you,"
she politely told the wolf.

Little Red Riding Hood waved good-bye
and continued on her way, singing.

"TRA! LA! LA! LA! LAAAAAAAAAAAAₐₐ!"

The wolf's tummy

RUMBLED and GRUMBLED!

He thought about all the DELICIOUS food he wanted to eat.

Fifteen sausages, eight pancakes, five ice cream cones, one big bag of potato chips, two birthday cakes, six chocolate bars, three tubs of popcorn, half a hot dog, one grandma and one girl in a little red riding hood.

WAIT, A MINUTE!

People aren't food.

Unless you're a hungry wolf...

The wolf knew EVERYTHING about the forest... and he also
knew a shortcut to Grandma's house.

When he reached the door, he shouted:

"WATCH OUT,
LITTLE RED RIDING HOOD'S GRANDMA!
I'M GOING TO
GOBBLE
YOU ALL UP!"

With this warning, Grandma leapt out
the window and hid in the bushes.

"DRATS!" the wolf said, when he found that
Grandma's house was empty.

So, he put on Grandma's clothes and hid in her bed. The wolf
was going to trick Little Red Riding Hood when she arrived.

Little Red Riding Hood arrived at Grandma's house, but Grandma did not seem like herself.

"What big **EYES** you have!"
gasped Little Red Riding Hood.

"All the better for **seeing** you!" replied the wolf in a silly voice.

"What big **EARS** you have!"
gasped Little Red Riding Hood.

"All the better for **hearing** you!" replied the wolf in a silly voice.

"And what big **TEETH** you have!"
gasped Little Red Riding Hood.

"ALL THE BETTER FOR EATING YOU!"

bellowed the wolf as he leapt out of bed.

Luckily, Little Red Riding Hood knew gymnastics.

She FLIPPED out the window and hid in the bushes. There, she found Grandma!

Soon, a cheerful lumberjack wandered past the bushes.

"PSSSSSSSSSSSSST!"

hissed Grandma. "Can you help us scare away a hungry
wolf who is hiding in my bed and wearing my clothes?"

"SURE!" said the cheerful lumberjack.
"I do that sort of thing ALL THE TIME!"

The cheerful lumberjack **crept** up to
the house and peered in the window.

Sure enough, the wolf was sound asleep in Grandma's bed.

"Awww, the little wolfie looks SO CUTE!"
said Little Red Riding Hood, peeping.

"CUTE?" replied Grandma.
"The little wolfie wants to EAT us!"

Little Red Riding Hood, Grandma and the cheerful lumberjack agreed that there was only ONE way to get rid of a hungry wolf...

So they crept into the house,

tiptoed

into the bedroom (where the wolf was sleeping) and shouted

"BOO!"

The hungry wolf
SQUEALED
and ran as fast as he could deep,
deep, **deep** into the forest.

Poor Grandma climbed back into bed. (She was feeling sick, remember?)

Together, Little Red Riding Hood, the cheerful lumberjack and Grandma enjoyed a small picnic on Grandma's bed.

Little Red Riding Hood was SO HAPPY, she started to sing.

"PICNIC! PICNIC! PICNIC! TRA-LA-LAAAAAAAAAA!"

Grandma and the cheerful lumberjack politely stuffed bread in their ears. **And the hungry wolf NEVER CAME BACK, EVER!**

First American Edition 2017
Kane Miller, A Division of EDC Publishing

Text, illustrations and design copyright © 2016 Hardie Grant Egmont
First published in Australia by Hardie Grant Egmont 2016

For information contact:
Kane Miller, A Division of EDC Publishing
PO Box 470663
Tulsa, OK 74147-0663
www.kanemiller.com
www.edcpub.com
www.usbornebooksandmore.com

Library of Congress Control Number: 2016943263

Printed in China
1 2 3 4 5 6 7 8 9 10

ISBN: 978-1-61067-610-6